From the dark mind of
Sea Caummisar

Painbows
&
Faded Tales

extreme horror

Copyright © 2022 by Sea Caummisar

All rights reserved. No portion of this book may be reproduced in any form without permission from the publisher, except as permitted by U.S. copyright law. For permissions contact sharoncheatham81@gmail.com

This is entirely a work of fiction, pulled out of my own imagination. All characters and events are not real (fictitious). If there are any similarities to real persons, living or dead, it is purely coincidental.

These are stories that are fake. Fiction. Yes, my mind may be a messed up place, or maybe it's an entertaining place. Take a walk with me, through my head, and witness my strange ways of thinking.

Description	4
This Book	6
Painbows	9
Penis Pumped	21
Dental Debacle	31
Garbage Man	39
A Few Previously Published Works	67
Intro to 'PGAD Anxiety'	68
The end notes from the dark mind of Sea Caummisar	70
PGAD Anxiety	71
Intro to 'Worst Fear'	80
Worst Fear	82
Intro to Drabbles	90
100 words Xmas Drabbles	92
Intro to Flash Fiction	97
Blood Wine	99
See ya next read	102

Description

Short story collection from the dark mind of Sea Caummisar.
Painbows
Penis Pumped
Dental Debacle
Garbage Man

Previously published works
PGAD Anxiety (published w/ 'The Absence of Pain')

Worst Fear (published in 'Books of Horror Community Anthology Vol.1')

100 word drabbles (published in 'Dark Xmas: Holiday Drabbles 100 Word Horror Stories')
- + The First Signs of a Serial Killer
- + A Perfect Snowman
- + A Bad Child
- + Rudolph the Bloody Nosed Reindeer
- + Shiny Ornaments

Blood Wine (flash fiction published in 'Dark Valentine Holiday Horror Collection: A Flash Fiction Anthology')

This Book

My informal greeting.

I have never released a book of short stories with the pseudonym Sea Caummisar, so I saw a need to rectify that situation.

As a writer, my computer is full of story ideas, half-written stories, etc… In all seriousness, I probably have more files of incomplete stories than I have completed. I have way more ideas jotted down than published. No napkin, notepad, post-it note, or even paper towel is safe in my house. I have literally woken up from dreams and scribbled story ideas on scrap paper on my bedside table (receipts included).

It's funny that when I left a notepad on my bedside table, I never had inspiring dreams. Then that notepad got moved because I needed to scribble down ideas during the day, and it ends up anywhere and everywhere around the house.

I won't even tell you how hard it is for me to find an ink pen when I need one. They seem to get lost in some abyss, never to be seen again. Crazy, huh? Yes. Sometimes I even wonder if my dogs have eaten them because the pens seem to vanish into thin air.

In all seriousness, my fur babies (both rescues; a brown boxer mix and a black lab mix) are taken care of. If I ever found them eating something that could harm them, I would stop them immediately. Maybe they hide my ink pens from me so I'll pet them more and work less?

I'm even good at texting myself story ideas if I'm on the go. Then those texts get buried by all my other texts. When the text message thing didn't work, I started posting ideas on my social media, but then setting them to private so that they're only visible to me.

I've had some crazy posts, that I didn't set the privacy correctly, that were all story ideas, but made all my friends worry about me. For example, I wanted to add a character (to 'Emetophilia') that saved all her tampons in a coffee tin. I had a few drinks, posted to my FB about saving tampons, didn't set the privacy correctly, and everyone wanted to know why in the world would I save my bloody tampons?!?!?

After that, things get awkward. I tell the social media commenters that it's a character idea, but I'm not so sure that they believed me. The post has since been set to where only I can view it, but still. Anyway, the yokes on them... (I'll show my age here) after menopause, I haven't needed a tampon for years!

Too much information? Yep. I'm sure it is.

You get the idea, right?

Some of these story ideas are inspired by reality, too. Real life can be crazier than fiction sometimes.

So I'm basically challenging myself to tidy some of those ideas up and publish some of them here as shorts.

Also, I have a few things that have been published in anthologies, and I plan on including those. Gasp! Oh, the horror! I have to face reality and realize that there are people out there who haven't read my every published word! Imagine that! It's crazy, right?

What exactly is a Painbow? Is it a word I made up? Does it have meaning? Maybe. Maybe not.

Welcome to 'Painbows and Faded Tales'.

A mixed-bag collection of the many ideas that invade my brain. It is labeled extreme, because a few stories are extreme. A few stories aren't.

If you're reading this, I'm welcoming you to take a journey through my head.

Here's your warning. Many of my thoughts are irregular. Abnormal. Uncomfortable. Possibly even non-linear. You can be the judge of that (which I'm sure you can tell by this intro that my brain is an absurd place).

Painbows

I see you eyeing my tattoos. There's a story that goes with'em.

Have you ever opened a beer bottle using someone's eye socket?

No, you say.

I have.

In all fairness, it was a twist off bottle. Good ole' American beer. Nothing sophisticated. Just watery slop with enough alcohol to give you a buzz if you drink enough of it.

It happened in a bar fight. The man picked a fight with me. I claimed self-defense, but the judge disagreed.

Dude was making fun of my nickname.

Hold on, give me a second, I'm getting there. Stop looking at my tats like that.

Let me tell this part first.

So dude at the bar, was name calling me and running his cum dumpster, if ya know what I mean. I approached him.

Once I was toe-to-toe with him, he sat down and shut up.

It was the way he sat down that struck a nerve. It was slow and disrespectful. Like one simple movement would make me forget what he was sayin'. Like if he turned away from me, his mean words would disappear.

The way he sat facing away from me.

Like a kid playing peek-a-boo, when they're not smart enough to realize that you can still see them, even if they can't see you.

I grabbed him by the back of his head and slammed his face down on the bar. According to the police report, that broke his nose. He had an unopened, cold brewski right there. I picked it up.

The angle of the headlock I had him in was perfect to stick that twist-off in his eye socket. It was soft and spongy. I really shoved the tip of the beer bottle up in there. Like farther than I thought I could.

When I couldn't shove it up there any further, I twisted. It was neat, feeling his skin twist with it.

Nope, I'm not crazy. I know I could feel his skin twisting because there was resistance.

You know what resistance is, right?

Okay. There was blood, too. Like dripping on my hand. That has to mean his skin twisted, right? Either that or those little ridges on the edges of the bottle cap. Maybe they ripped his skin. Those suckers are hard.

Could be a weapon, I suppose. The judge says the beer bottle was a weapon. I say it was merely a refreshment.

The lid came off.

And I have to say, that douche's blood made that beer taste better.

That's what he got for running his mouth.

I doubt that would work with the kinds of bottles that don't twist off.

What do you think?

Why are you so quiet?

At least you're not eyeing my tats anymore.

I've had plenty of time in this jail cell to think about this.

The other kinds of beer bottles. The fancy ones. The ones I can't even pop off with my teeth. I think I could get that work with an eye socket.

Yeah, I know it sounds crazy, but just hear me out here.

What if you shoved up under the bone. Ya know, that bone above your eye. The one right under your eyebrow.

Good. You're paying attention. I see you rubbing that bone right now.

There's enough space that you could wedge that bottle up in there. One of two things would happen.

10

Either the flesh would tear and bone would chip away, or it would pop off the bottle cap.

I'd love to try.

Even if the bone chipped off, I think I'd try again.

Maybe with a different angle. Maybe with a harder tug. There are many variables when popping open a beer. I would make it work, or I would keep trying until the bone was nothing but fragments floating around inside his skin.

Now you're looking at me like I'm crazy. I guess I got sidetracked. Oh, yeah, thanks for the reminder.

My nickname. Rainbows.

Yes, he did lose his eye. Why else would I get sentenced to spend a year here? Yeah, my lawyer was pretty good. I'll be out in half that time, he says.

Are you keeping up with the story? I'm done talking about eyes and beer bottles. You asked about my nickname, right? Or was it my tats? I forget.

Moving on.

I was five, maybe six, maybe seven-years-old. My old man was sitting on the porch with his usual bunch of dudes, the ones I always called uncle, even though they weren't no blood kin.

They were playing dominoes. They never let me play.

No big deal, but I got to play in the front yard. It had just finished raining, and the grass was wet. I climbed a tree, chased a cat, typical kid stuff.

But I looked up in the sky that day and saw the prettiest thing ever.

Not only one, but two, rainbows. Have you ever seen dual rainbows? One is big, one is small. The small one looks like an echo of the larger one.

It amazed me.

I pointed up, because I knew I couldn't be selfish and not share this sight with other people. I had to, it was my duty, to tell other people, so that they could see this too.

It truly was an amazing sight. A wonder. Does that make sense?

So I'm pointing up, and I say, "Rainbows! Rainbows!".

I'll never forget the look on my dad's face.

He stopped the game by slamming down a domino. I swear I saw all the other tiles bounce up in the air off the table.

Then my uncles were just looking at him like he was crazy or something.

I guess to get the full story, you had to be there. But my dad was notorious for wearing those white tank tops, designed to be worn under shirts. That was my dad's entire wardrobe. Wife beaters, as they call them, and blue jeans. The baggy kind, always worn lower than his waistline. Never wore a shirt over those tank tops, like they were intended to be worn.

My dad went away for months at a time and would always return buff. Like bulging muscles. As an adult, I know now he would go to jail. Use the gym daily. Get out. Come home. Commit some crime. Go back to jail. It was a never-ending cycle.

So he spent a lot of time at the gym.

Plus, he shaved his head. All the way to his scalp. The top of his head was always shining, I guess from sweat. Or maybe he put oil or some kind of wax to get that sheen. I'll never know.

Back to the story. So dad slams down a domino, stops the game and stands.

All my uncles with eyes on him. They all dressed like him. Even shaved their heads, too.

Back to where I was.

My dad's upper lip curled. "Are you queer, boy?"

I was so young, I didn't know what queer meant, so I didn't know how to respond. Of course, I know what it means now, but the way my dad said it, I thought it was a bad word. I learned better now. It's a lifestyle. To each their own.

I've even been known to be gay for the stay, so I see no problems with that lifestyle.

But my old school, gangster dad…

Well, he used it as an insult.

I'm standing there, frozen in time.

Like watching a movie in slow motion. My dad was coming towards me, down the porch steps. One at a time.

I knew I should answer him. Otherwise, I'd feel his wrath in the form of some sort of physical abuse.

"I think the rainbows are pretty." I'm still pointing up to the sky, praying and hoping that my dad would look up and see what I saw.

If he only looked up, he'd see this wonderful array of colors in the clouds.

He never looked up.

Instead, he grabbed me by my arm, and jerked my feet off the ground. "Boy, I'm gonna beat you until you piss in your pants."

You know what he did?

He commenced to beating on me. Swatting my backside, my feet dangling, pain erupting from my shoulder as he held me off the ground. I just knew my arm would break off at any given moment.

I suppose he could have been going for my backside. That's where my mom would always spank me. On my bottom.

But dad kept missing the mark.

His hand landed on my back, right in the middle. I'm squirming and all, hoping he'd release me.

I'm crying, begging him to stop.

My uncles were laughing at me from the porch, making everything worse. That could have been the first time that I truly felt shame. Embarrassed is an understatement. The men I've always idolized were getting a good laugh at me being a sissy. Another word my father insulted me with, often.

Snot is bubbling out of my nose. Tears are rolling down my cheeks.

Then he started with the closed fists. Maybe to my kidneys. Looking back, I'm pretty sure it was my kidneys. I didn't know it at the time. I only knew it hurt.

If you've been paying attention, my dad's muscles weren't only for appearance. They gave him strength, too.

I'm begging. Crying. Pleading for him to stop.

He kept on beating me.

My dad was the kind of man that didn't like repeating himself. I knew that if I thought hard enough, I could fix this. And it wouldn't be by pointing at the rainbows.

Remember? He told me he'd beat me til I pissed myself.

That's all I had to do to stop the pain.

Do you know how hard it is to pee, suspended in the air?

I tried as hard as I could, but I couldn't go.

I had to picture myself in a standing position, pulling my child sized pecker from my pants before I could force the urine out of me.

Hey, are you paying attention? I'm not finished yet.

After several minutes, which felt like an eternity, I felt my pants get warm. My favorite short pants. Mom picked 'em out for me. They were light gray. She said it was a neutral color. I could wear any shirt with them.

My crotch gets hot, and my uncles start laughing louder.

I felt it running down my legs, dripping in my shoes. I could smell it, too.

Dad released his grip and I fell down in the wet grass, all muddy and crap. I knew mom would now spank me for dirtying up my clothes, but she only ever hit my butt. And she wasn't as strong as my dad.

I'm on the ground, perched up on my elbows, looking up to see my dad, who was now rubbing his shoulder! Like he was the one in pain! As if dangling me in the air and hitting me hurt him!

Above his shiny head, I saw those pretty rainbows.

Maybe it was God's way of reminding me how small I was. How small all of us are. No matter what, I could never make a rainbow, but Mother Nature could.

It truly was a beautiful sight.

Mom comes out and starts fussing at dad.

She was actually gentle with me when she rolled me over.

Her eyes landed on my gray pants, covered in urine and mud.

"Red? What'd you do, Razor? He's pissing blood. Ya know, we ain't have the money to take him to the hospital."

That was her concern. Money.

My uncles weren't laughing now.

Mom was crazy like that. Maybe she'd pull out a gun and shoot them. Or poison the snacks she'd make for'em. Who knew with her? Unpredictable. That was my mother. Except when it came to me. She was always kind to me. Except when she swatted my backside.

That was the only person my dad was nice towards. Why? I'll never know.

I pointed up, because I was still in awe of the wonder floating in the sky. It kept my mind off my physical pain. Mother nature was letting me know that I wasn't alone and that the world was full of beauty.

Mom did look up. I guess she was curious what I was pointing towards.

"Oh, pretty."

That's all she said.

My dad wraps his arm around her shoulders, and finally looks up. "Yeah, it is."

A police car rolled up in front of the house. I'm not sure why. Maybe a neighbor saw the incident and called them. Maybe the cop just happened to be driving by. I guess I'll never know.

Dad went back to jail.

I never saw mom again either.

The cops took me to the hospital, where a nice doctor fixed me up.

Then a nice social worker came in, and found me a new place to live.

I'll never forget that rainbow. It's my last memory of my folks. My happy memories keep me going in this place.

Hence, all my rainbow tats.

For some reason, people still called me rainbows. Even the uncles I'd see from time to time on the streets.

As I got older, that name evolved to Painbows.

Why? Not sure.

I guess people don't pick their own nicknames.

That's just the way life is.

So yeah, the way you were looking at my tats, was the same way that guy in the bar did.

Are you tracking me?

Ya know, the reason why I'm in here. Self-defense against the prick who wanted to make fun of my tats. The human beer bottle opener.

No, he wasn't the first.

Why are you looking away now?

I pour my soul out to my new cellmate, and you get all quiet?

Maybe it's for the best. The last guy talked too much.

I'm full of stories.

You seem to be a good listener.

You have anything to say about my tats?

Nope. Didn't think so. Most people don't anymore.

We got nothing better to do. Might as well tell some stories.

Penis Pumped

One of the things about working in an adult toy store is that you become desensitized to things that other people would find unusual. If a customer came in and asked me about any type of vibrator, it was my job to know which ones would suit their needs.

Want a vibrator with different speeds? I'll point you in the right direction. Need clitoral and g-spot stimulation? We sold many of those. New to anal beads but were curious? I know a perfect starter set for you. Or maybe you've used anal beads so often that you need an upgrade? I had just the thing for you.

Panties worn by your partner, but you hold the remote control? We have those, too. With a push of a button, your partner could have an orgasm under the dinner table, unbeknownst to the others dining with you. A fun game played by lovers.

Tired of masturbating in a sock? Even though I'm female, I know which pocket pussies sold the best and the ones customers sought out the most. I was even up to date on the reviews; oral and otherwise (usually from male co-workers).

Surprisingly, life sized sex dolls didn't sell too often. Maybe it was the price point. Expensive. Maybe people didn't want to have to hide a human-sized toy in their home. That will still remain a mystery to me.

Those were common requests. The normal stuff.

Usually, people just wanted orgasms and the typical feel good stimulation. I could talk sex toys with the best of them. It was our job when we got a new product to learn everything it was capable of. Some we even tested ourselves.

Overall, it was a fun job.

It was rare though that a customer would come in with a request that would tug at my heart strings. Like I said, I was desensitized. I judged nobody. Felt nothing. It was work.

As with any job, it becomes routine and uneventful.

There was one customer that I'll never forget.

The man rolled into the store in a motorized wheelchair. A fancy one. It fitted his fancy van out in the parking lot that was custom made for him and his disability. I had watched from the cash register as the man parked (CCTV camera) and a ramp lowered him and his wheelchair.

Other than another customer having to hold the door open for him, the man was self-sufficient.

His face was unfamiliar, so I didn't strike up a conversation with him like I would the regulars. We had many regulars due to the large movie theater that played pornography twenty-fours hours a day. Seven days a week. We even had private booths in the back with small screens that would play porn when you inserted a coin.

I won't get started on the glory holes. I always felt bad for the janitor that had to clean up those messes.

The man in the wheelchair comes in, and I'm friendly, but not overly. There was a tact to making someone feel welcome but not on display. You'd be surprised how many people were embarrassed to even walk in an adult bookstore, nevertheless make a purchase.

I gave him a nod and the standard you'd find in any store. "If you need any help, feel free to ask me anything." A sales person, but not pushy.

The man's face blushed red, but spoke. "Penis pumps?"

I pointed to the penis pump aisle. "If you need assistance, I'll be more than glad to help."

The man didn't speak again, but with a push of a button, his chair was off to his destination.

You would think that purchasing a penis pump would be an easy task, but with so many options, I understand why it could be overwhelming. They varied in size, suction power, and ease of use.

I watched the man, but not obviously. Looking at him from my peripheral vision, I could tell he was confused.

The man stared at the many items on display, and after several minutes, he reached out for one. It was on one of the higher display shelves and his arm was stretched as far as it could, but couldn't grasp the one he desired.

From the corner of my eye, I saw him look in my direction.

Casually, I turned and made eye contact. "Is there something I can help you with, sir?"

"Please." The man was polite.

From where I stood, I couldn't tell which item he wanted, but when I approached him, I saw that he was reaching for the most expensive penis pump. Some people think a higher price means higher quality. That's not always true, but in this case, it was.

"You have a good eye," I noted as I grabbed the product for him. "This one has several suction intensities. Powered by a wall plug, even an adaptor to plug into a cigarette lighter in a vehicle. The only setback is that this brand sells their c-rings separately."

"C-ring?"

His question was brief, but it was apparent he had no clue what I was talking about. "A cock ring."

He still looked puzzled, so I elaborated. I wasn't shy, but hoped my frank language didn't bother him. Cock wasn't a word you'd use in everyday conversation with a stranger. Unless you were me.

"Many men use cock rings with the penis pump. Depends on what you're looking for. I've been told, many men enjoy the sensation of the suction. Others do it for enlargement. The cock ring helps with that. You place the ring around the shaft of the pump, and when you reach your desired size, you slide the ring down to the base of your penis. That traps the blood, keeping the erection firm."

The man spoke quietly, I assume so other customers wouldn't hear him, but he replied. "It's not for me. I'm paralyzed from my waist down. Numb. No feeling or movement at all. It's more for my wife. I want to please her."

Believe it or not, it was probably the sweetest thing I'd ever heard in that store. This man was not making a purchase for his own gratification. It was for his wife. If he truly had no feeling, the act of sex wouldn't give him pleasure.

"So you'd need a cock ring. No worries, I can help you with that."

The man proceeded with his purchase. Didn't speak much unless it was a question about the how-to's of working his new toy.

For some reason, he left an impression on me.

From the CCTV, I watched the man rolling out to his fancy van, but now he had a smile on his face, in contrast to the look of embarrassment I saw in the store.

That was my good deed for the day. So I thought.

It wasn't every day that job gave me warm feelings of being helpful.

I went back to work. I greeted a customer. Rang one of up. Had a conversation about the weather with a regular customer leaving the theater. Normal job stuff.

When I glanced at the camera screen, the van was still in the parking lot.

I didn't think much of it because I wasn't sure what the man had to do once he was inside the van to get in a driving position. I figured he was just busy wrangling his way into the driver seat. I honestly had no clue what the ergonomics were of a custom van for a person paralyzed from the waist down.

But I was curious, so I watched. From the camera angle, I couldn't see inside the vehicle.

I did see a customer, a regular, park next to the van, get out of his car, look inside the van window and run inside the store.

"Call 911! Right now!"

Calling emergency services wasn't a normal part of our job. Even if there was a fight in the store, or even a theft, security were the ones to get the situation under control. The customers wouldn't take too kindly to police showing up if they were in a theater, maybe touching themselves (shaking hands with the milkman), or whatever.

Discretion was a code we lived by.

"The van! Outside! He's screaming for help! He needs an ambulance!"

My heart fell. I had this bad feeling in my gut, probably worse because I knew the paralyzed man was so polite and kind. Calling an ambulance wouldn't guarantee that police would show up, but it was a possibility.

My manager poked his head out of a small office after hearing the commotion. I knew this wasn't my decision to make. That's why managers got paid more. To make the hard decisions.

My manager rushed outside, ran to the van, and looked inside. Even tried to open a door, but it must have been locked. He knew I was watching so he gave a thumbs up symbol.

While I was scrambling my brain trying to figure out if a thumbs up meant to make the phone call, or if a thumbs up meant the man in the van was fine, my manager ran in. "Make the call now!"

I picked up the phone to dial in a panic.

My manager took the phone. I'm being selfish here, because I was relieved. Not only would I not be on the hook for making the call to emergency services if the higher ups frowned on the decision, but also because it meant I could go out in the parking lot and see for myself what the fuss was all about.

By the time I made it out there, a couple customers were looking in the van window. Both males. Each with looks of disgust on their faces. One hunched over, his hands on his knees like he might vomit. The other had his hands on his crotch in a protective gesture.

I made myself a spot between the two.

I looked in the van window.

I almost wish that I never had.

The penis pump was plugged into the vehicle's cigarette lighter.

This was many years ago, when cars still had those.

The cord ran from the cigarette lighter to the penis pump.

The penis pump was attached to the man's penis.

Like I said earlier, this was an expensive, high-powered penis pump.

Typically, a man would feel when his man parts became too swollen.

It would be painful, and they'd power off the device.

A paralyzed man would not feel that pressure of blood filling their sex organ.

The nice customer couldn't feel it, but his penis enlarged to the point of explosion. He couldn't have felt it or he would have shut the equipment down before causing too much damage.

He was screaming, but maybe that was a psychological thing, because he was seeing the same thing we all saw.

Inside the clear tube of the penis pump was nothing but clumps of broken away flesh. Blood dripped from the receptacle. And there was lots of it.

I'll never forget the moment he raised the toy away from his body.

What was left of his stump, which wasn't much, looked like an overcooked hot dog. Like a weiner that had been fried too hard and split down the middle. Random chunks of meat blown away, some still inside the tube of the pump.

As he pulled the toy off, a clump of mangled muscle elongated, the tissue still spongy and pliable. A ribbon of gore drooping down after losing suction and bouncing slightly until it landed in a heap of carnage atop his scrotum.

I'm talking a puddle of blood twirling on his hairy ball sac.

Talk about a horrible sight!

I'll never forget that nice customer.

The ambulance came, and luckily the police didn't. They rushed him to the hospital.

I don't know what became of that man, but I never did see him in the store. Never again.

By the way, are you in the market for a penis pump? I know of one in particular that is super high powered.

++++++

A note from the dark mid of Sea Caummisar

Would you believe me if I said this was a true story? That it happened years ago before everything was powered by rechargeable USB ports. Probably not. That's fair.

But I'll never forget it.

Dental Debacle

The teeth whitening kits sold at the drug stores only worked so well.

Sean was slathering some gel on his front teeth when a sharp pain radiated from his gum line, ending in his nostril, resulting in him reaching for his mouth and closing his lip. Not only did it hurt, the gel made a mess inside the pouch of his lip.

"Dammit!" he cursed himself in the mirror. The several minutes he spent applying the product had been a waste. The kit wasn't cheap, either, so he wasn't in a hurry to go out and buy more.

The pain was now more of a tingle, but an annoyance all the same.

Being at the age when a few gray hairs started to sprout, and a few faint wrinkles were forming around his eyes, his yellow teeth bothered him. The reflection looked older than he wanted to appear.

As a child, his mother was adamant about visiting the dentist regularly. Two years of his teenage prime was spent with braces on his teeth. Regular brace tightenings and cleanings with the orthodontist weren't the worst of it. It was the nicknames the schoolyard bullies dubbed him.

Metal mouth, brace face, train tracks.

He heard them all through his childhood.

Not to mention that his first girlfriend refused to kiss her with her tongue, for fear she would cut herself on his dental appliance.

As he grew older, Sean appreciated his straight teeth. The bullies from his childhood never saw the handsome man he grew into and the way the females flocked to him. His straight, white teeth contributed to his success with the ladies.

He'd even recalled an article where he read something along the lines that sexual attraction was human instinct and good teeth activated some sort of breeding gene within women. From what he gathered, it was automatic, and the woman might not even be aware of it, but they wanted to carry the babies of a man from 'good stock'. Healthy genetics, good looks, pheromones; all of those things played their part.

But straight, white teeth were a factor.

Sean wasn't in the business of having babies, but he loved the process of making babies.

Being a single man, never married in his four decades, was a conscious choice he made.

Age was not on his side.

Not only did a few gray hairs and slight wrinkles take away from his looks, so did his yellow teeth. It was putting a damper on his dating lifestyle.

Using a piece of toilet paper, Sean tried to wipe some of the messy whitening gel from his lip, but the paper crumbled like an overused eraser, making an even bigger mess.

Gargling from a glass of cold water reactivated the severe, sharp pain stemming from the gum line of his front teeth.

It had been far too long since he'd made a trip to the dentist.

Years ago, he'd had a root canal performed, and swore to himself that he would never return to the dentist. It wasn't necessarily painful, it was the feeling of the pressure building up between his ears that he hated. When they cleaned his teeth, the high-pitched sound of the scraper digging in the hard crevices of his mouth made him want to jump out of his skin. An internal echo ringing in his ears that still haunted him.

Also, he remembered how it felt breathing, like he was choking, despite the fact that his mouth had been wide open. Maybe too wide, and he blamed the dentist for that. He recalled how the corners of his lips felt like they were cracking.

Memories of the dentist were not happy.

Staring at his yellow teeth, and now a painful orifice, was enough motivation for him to make an appointment with a dentist. But not without having a proper plan.

++++++

Sean sat in a small room, staring out a glass window at a beautiful, sunny day. It was a serene scene if you could overlook the steady flow of traffic.

"Long time no see, Mr, Russel," the man in the white lab coat entered and looked up from a clipboard, greeting him with a warm smile. "Let's get you seated."

The chair itself looked very inviting and comfortable.

Sean slid his legs over the long curvature of the seat, leaned back and relaxed.

Staring down at him was a large light attached to a movable fixture.

It took everything in him to not peek at the array of tools on the dentist's desk.

The anti-anxiety medicine that Sean typically used to help him sleep was coming in handy. Every muscle in his body was loose, and his thoughts seemed to float above him. Closing his eyes helped, and he thought he could even go to sleep.

"Mr. Russel, it says here you're having sharp pains, from your upper front tooth? You are also interested in having a cleaning? And whitening?"

"Yes, sir." The words fell from Sean's mouth easily. He didn't have a care in the world.

"Open wide, let me have a look," the dentist said, leaning forward.

His eyes were closed, but Sean thought he heard something squeaking. *That's the light. I think he's moving the light. That's all that is.*

There was another sound, like metal clanging together. Another sound of the dentist's stool rolling across the floor.

That sound isn't in my head. Not yet, at least. I think he scooted and then grabbed something from his arsenal of tools.

"Aha!"

Sean tried to speak, but realized there was something in his mouth, holding it open. Maybe it was the dentist's hand. He was too relaxed to really know.

"How's this feel, Mr. Russel?"

It was the familiar scraping sound he recalled from prior visits, but this time, it didn't bother Sean in the least. His mind was elsewhere, still picturing the view he had from the window. The shining sun and how green the trees were this time of year. *This isn't bad at all. I should have thought to take my anxiety meds before every dentist visit. This is the way to do it.*

"Mr. Russel, if the discomfort gets unbearable, let me know, I could numb an area if I have to."

Since he couldn't speak, Sean gave a thumbs up gesture. The universal sign that he was fine, seemed to please the doctor.

Not fully knowing what the dentist was doing, nor caring, Sean was so relaxed he was almost asleep. Sounds were non-existent. Nothing was painful. He was in bliss.

Until the dentist screamed. "Oh shit!"

Pulled from his slumber, Sean opened his eyes to see a look of terror on the dentist's face, who was staring at the large window. Seconds passed quickly, too fast to acknowledge what was happening.

From the corner of the eye, the last thing Sean saw was a blur of movement, a car barreling into the wall. A force of gravity crashing into him. Glass shattering, bricks crumbling, and lifting his body and slamming into him and pinning him to his death.

Damn.

+++++

Afterthoughts from the dark mind of Sea Caummisar….

Who is familiar with urban legends? Or perhaps it's folklore? Stories passed through word of mouth… the kind of stories that get told so many times that the facts change slowly, a little bit, w/ each retelling. Before the internet, it wasn't as easy as hopping online and performing a fact check.

When I was a child (I'm in my 40's now), there was a story about a car accident. The car accident did happen. It was a single car accident, and the car skidded off the road when the car in front of them suddenly slammed on their brakes. Instead of slamming into the car in front of them, the driver veered off road. The car was stopped by some sort of an embankment, on the edge of a parking lot.

That parking lot was a dentist office.

That is what inspired me to write this story. No, the car did not hit the dental office in real life, but it came super close.

Could you imagine getting work done in your mouth and a car driving through the building and killing you?

Many people already have anxiety and fear of going to the dentist.

In that little short piece, I wanted it known that Sean feared the dentist, but found a way to cope with it. (Anti-anxiety meds.)

So he was scared, got there, and found out it wasn't so bad being medicated… then BOOM> he's dead out of nowhere. Probably not even with enough time to realize how or why.

That's life. It's when you find ways to cope, ways to feel comfortable, but out of nowhere, your entire world can change.

But the interesting part of the story (from when I was a child) was that the female passenger must have been pleasuring her husband, the driver, orally, because she bit IT off. By IT, I mean his man parts. Everyone from that area heard about the accident, but somehow it got turned into a sex thing. Is it true? I'll never know. But that story has stuck w/ me for some time now.

I suppose I could have written a story about fellatio while driving, but those stories are overdone. They all end the same. She usually bites it off. Big shocker. Instead, I wrote the story from inside the dentist office.

Garbage Man

The job wasn't so bad. Especially when it was done in one of the new fancy trucks. The vehicles with the robot arms that would come down and pick up the trash bin were easy, if you knew what you were doing. It took some finesse to line it up properly. Once you mastered that, you were golden.

If not, you would have a major mess on your hands.

There were a surprisingly high number of people who chose not to discard their trash in bags.

Wade's truck was in the shop getting work done on the brakes, and he was stuck with one of the older garbage truck models. The kind that you had to physically lift the rubbish bin, turn it upside down, and shake out the contents.

Bags were so easy. They'd flow out of the container easily.

If people didn't use bags, items would tend to try and blow away in the wind. Receipts, paper, fast food wrappers, newspaper scraps, etc...

Technically, it was Wade's job to chase down any item that didn't land in the truck, but he was feeling lazy today.

It was hot, and his thick gloves were making his hands sweaty.

If he was ever asked his occupation, he would reply by saying sanitation engineer. His co-workers always told him that was misleading, but Wade thought it was better than the alternative.

When he used to tell people that he was a trash collector, he tired of people always asking how much his job stank.

To him, the stink wasn't the hard part. Odors were something one could get used to. Wade was aware of his nose blindness, but the smell hardly ever bothered him.

The hard part was the physical labor. If and when he got stuck in an old truck that required physical lifting, and the occasional tracking down of garbage fluttering in the wind, he hated his job.

The shifts were always with two employees.

One would drive.

The other would have a place to stand on the backside, and a handle to hold onto, as the driver drove. The one standing on the back would drop off the truck, lift the cans, empty them, and climb back up.

Over and over.

Many times a day.

The man Wade usually worked with was willing to rotate roles. They'd take turns, every hour, one driving, the other doing the physical labor.

Not the old timer that Wade was working with today. The older garbage collector would only drive, always throwing his seniority and years of hard work in the younger man's face.

Wade pulled a sweaty glove off and wiped his face with it, realizing too late that he had wiped some sort of garbage goo on his face. The removed glove was also a tool to swat away pesky flies, swarming in circles above the garbage. Looking at the glove, he assumed it to be a combination of coffee grinds, cigarette ashes, and some sort of sticky fluid.

In times like now, Wade would remind himself that the job paid well. Especially considering that it took basically no skill. Definitely no schooling.

When he first started the job, he was shocked to learn that he had to take an ethics class prior to being hired. It was what Wade called 'mumbo-jumbo BS'. He knew he had common sense and knew it wasn't polite to look in people's discarded trash.

Mail was the main topic of the ethics class.

A surprisingly large number of people would toss out mail with their personal information, or financial details, not fearing identity theft. Apparently, a garbage man had been fired prior to Wade's employment for stealing people's personal details.

One bad apple in the bunch, and everyone had to suffer the consequence of sitting through a boring ethics class.

There was also a class about safety and ways to not get hurt on the job.

Wade prided himself for excelling at all the required courses, and would tell anyone who put down a garbage man's role that there was much more to the job than they realized. It was a great topic at parties.

Before he started telling people he was a sanitation engineer, and used the term trash man, he heard all the nonsense common people associated with the job.

'You pick up garbage! That must stink bad!'

'Why would you choose that job? A monkey could do it!'

'I thought I smelled something bad!'

So many negative stereotypes came with the occupation.

Wade climbed back onto the back step of the truck, gave the driver a thumbs up, and they drove to the next house.

Wade climbed down, his face still sticky from wiping it with the filthy glove, and picked up a garbage can. He flipped the lid off and as he raised it, a stench he had never experienced assaulted his nostrils.

The ethics courses had taught him it was not polite to ever look inside someone's trash, but curiosity got the better of him. The rancid aroma almost made him gag, which was something Wade hadn't experienced ever since he was new to the job.

Moldy food. Decayed meat. Even when it was infested by wriggling maggots. Dirtied baby diapers. Dead fish. Wade's nose was blind to all of these smells. Also, a strong stomach to boot. Smells didn't bother Wade at all.

This was different. Raunchy. Unique. Unfamiliar. Intriguing. Stimulating. Interesting.

Unlike anything else he had ever smelled before in the back of the truck.

And this odor was coming through a tied-plastic bag.

Wade's thick gloves made it almost impossible to tear through the plastic. It kept stretching, refusing to rip.

He had to remove the glove and poke it with a finger.

He glanced up and saw the driver's scrunched-up face looking aggravated in the side mirror.

Time wasn't on Wade's side and he knew he had to hurry.

The bag finally tore, releasing a more pungent scent. One so strong that it made Wade's eyes water.

Between a mound of bones, possibly chicken, and a sock with a hole in it was what looked like a nipple staring back at him, if the nipple had been left in the heat of the sun to wither. If the nipple was shriveled atop a purplish heap of meat.

Wade blinked and couldn't help himself, but he poked it, and despite the puckered flesh, it wiggled like a real breast. The jagged edges of the mass were coated with thick layers of redness, so dark and crimson that they looked like dark, liquified rubies

Peering around the edge of the truck, Wade looked up and saw the driver throw his hands in the air out of frustration. The vehicle window lowered, and the driver stuck his head out. "What are you doing back there? The sooner you get done, the sooner we get to go home. I have plans tonight."

Staring back at the object that Wade thought was a detached breast, he threw the bag into the back of the truck and watched as it blended in with all the other disposed of waste.

Wade looked at the house, memorized the address, and climbed back up, and gave a thumbs up. It was time to repeat the garbage collecting process.

++++

As with any other professional job, Wade only worked five days a week.

Having the freedom to enjoy his weekends was a perk of the job. Unless there was a holiday. In that case, he would work an occasional Saturday, but that wasn't very often.

Curiosity was still eating at him. His mind was wondering what his eyes had seen.

If he had abided by his training, he would have had the driver also look at the item, and see if what he thought he was seeing was a reality. If so, and if both parties were in agreement that they were indeed looking at a discarded body part, it was their duty to report it to the authorities.

Wade hadn't done that.

Firstly, he and the driver didn't have a great relationship. If it hadn't been a woman's breast, the driver would have chastised him for wasting time. The old timer never wanted to climb down out of the driver seat, anyway.

Secondly, what if it had been a breast? What if the owner of the refused trash saw him peeking in the bag? If authorities had been notified, a killer could have possibly seen him, making him an instant enemy.

If it hadn't been a breast, the authorities would have laughed at him.

Wade was tired of people laughing at him. Especially about his preferred occupation.

It wasn't only curiosity that was eating him alive. It was all of his training that made him extra aware that it was his civic duty to keep the community safe from a butcher that was removing body parts from females.

Wade waited until after dark, not worrying about having to wake early the next morning to go to work. With a gun attached to his hip, he drove to the house, careful to park far enough away to not be seen approaching a side window on foot.

It was dark in between the houses. There was a sidewalk, the grass mowed and tidy, leading from the front porch to a back door.

Wade's nerves were shot, but he wouldn't allow himself to back out of doing this. If he did this, if he had discovered a murderer, if he could take a murderer off the streets, he would have much more to talk about at parties than his job.

Also, he could be declared a hero, erasing the stain that his job marked upon his reputation.

There were several lights on in the house, making it easy to look inside.

After ensuring he couldn't be seen from the street, Wade stood on the tips of his toes, his nose barely high enough to reach the bottom of the window.

The window shades were angled in the way Roman blinds usually are. Slats upon slats, slanted so that if Wade looked upward, he could see inside, but only in small sections and at a weird angle.

From where he stood, he had a good, clear vision of the white ceiling, and Wade moved to another window. The next one was much lower, and the shades were angled downward, giving him a clear view of the carpet.

He heard a voice. Male. "I'm just in the kitchen. Need anything while I'm in here?."

Another voice spoke back. Female. "I need water with my pills."

"Okay."

The fact nobody was screaming in pain gave him a feeling of relief. If anything, the voices he heard were kind and caring. Shrugging off what he thought he saw in the garbage can, Wade turned to leave. As nice as it would have been to be a hero, it felt better knowing that he hadn't seen anything suspicious in their trash.

The female voice spoke again. "Honey, I need more bandages, too. It won't stop bleeding."

Wade was confused. What wouldn't stop bleeding? And why would she need bandages unless she was injured?

Following the sounds of the female voice, Wade stumbled across a third window. A white, fluffy cat had its head stuck between the shades, creating an opening for Wade to look inside.

In the center of the room was a hospital bed, a woman lying in it. The head of the bed was raised and she had both hands on her chest, dabbing the area with a cloth.

Wade watched from his side view as she raised the white cloth, now stained red.

The woman turned her head towards another room, blocked by a wall that Wade couldn't see.

"Honey, we need to do this quicker than we thought. Can we do it again? Same as last night?"

The man's voice hesitated. "You sure? I don't know if that's a good-"

"I'm sure!" the woman replied, her voice raised.

From the weird angle of the slants, he saw a pair of legs enter the room, a large hand holding a large butcher knife. "I don't know, honey." The hand and knife moved up and down with each word the man spoke.

Suddenly, the cat jumped down from the window sill, and the man turned his head, catching Wade's shocked face through the glass.

Wade's fight or flee instinct kicked in because he thought about running, but quickly changed his mind. This was his moment to do something brave. Something no other garbage man had never done before.

Instead, he grabbed for his gun and had it pointed through the glass, aimed at the man, now looking outside.

"I'm calling the police!" Wade warned.

The man used one hand to keep the blinds open, and the other hand dropped the blade. The man raised it above his head, in a non-threatening gesture.

Wade felt his hip, but his phone wasn't attached to his belt clip. In his haste to solve the mystery of what he had seen in the garbage, he must have left his cell phone at home.

The man inside nodded his head. "Okay. That's fine."

"No, it's not," the woman sat higher in the hospital bed. "Why would he do that?"

"I don't know, hon. There's a crazy man outside with a gun. A peeping tom. I'd be glad if the police arrived."

"Is this some trickery?" Wade questioned. "What's going on here?"

"Get away from the window! He can't shoot you if you don't stand there!"

The man moved out of view, and Wade was now more confused than ever.

Wade was staring at what he could see of the woman's face, which was hollow and frail. Large, black bags beneath her eyes highlighted how bloodshot they were. The bones of her concave cheeks were evident, with paper thin flesh barely covering them.

She spoke. "Go! Whatever you do, don't let him call the police!"

Not sure what to do, Wade contemplated turning to leave, but also too curious to do so. It was only seconds before he heard a familiar click behind him, the cocking of the hammer of a pistol.

"I don't know what you think you're doing, you peeping tom, but I suggest you drop the weapon before I spray your brains all over my house! This is America and I have the right to defend my home."

Being at the disadvantage of having a gun pointed at the backside of his head, Wade contemplated how quickly he could turn around, raise his own gun, and shoot the man.

While Wade was busy thinking, he felt something small poke him in the back of his neck (maybe a needle). Within seconds, his world went black and Wade's body crumpled to the ground.

++++

When Wade woke up, the bright light blinded him. In reaction, he tried to raise his hands to his eyes and shield them, but found that he was handcuffed to the arms of a chair. His head was swimming and dazed with confusion.

His eyes landed on the woman in the bed, her chest now covered with fresh bandages.

"Roy, he's awake!" the woman yelled. "I don't know who you are, or what you're doing outside my window, but I swear to Christ that-"

The man came into the room quickly. "Honey, calm on down. I'll deal with him. You don't need to get yourself worked up over nothing."

"Nothing? You call that nothing? I call it perfect timing so that I can-"

The man sat on the edge of the hospital bed and gently cradled the woman's hand. "Honey, you're safe now. No need to get all upset. You need to relax." Roy's eyes shifted to Wade, and his light-hearted smile turned immediately into a scowl. "What are you doing peeking in my windows? Threatening me with a gun?"

Wade gulped so hard he felt a bubble roll down his dry throat. "I came to save the lady. I saw- I thought I saw - no, I did see her breast in the trash and came to rescue her."

"You're digging through my trash, too? What kind of pervert are you?" Roy asked.

"I'm not a pervert! I'm a sanitation engineer."

The man and woman looked at each other with quizzical expressions, so Wade elaborated. "I'm a garbage man. You put it in the garbage! What was I to think?" His hands started shaking, clinking the handcuffs against the chair.

The woman looked down at her bandage. "No. That's impossible. You ate it, right, Roy? I watched you eat it!"

"I did, hon. You watched me."

"What?" Wade was more confused now than ever.

Roy's hardened expression softened slightly. "You're a garbage man. What a rotten job. You thought I was in here cutting up women and you came to be some sort of vigilante champion?"

Wade felt the need to defend his choice of occupation. "There's nothing wrong with my job, until I find a discarded body part."

"Why didn't you call the police?" Roy asked with sincerity. "If you thought a law was being broken, why not call the authorities? Which, by the way, no law was being broken."

Wade had his reasons for not calling the police and for not getting a second opinion from the garbage truck driver, but now they felt unimportant.

"Right," the woman chimed in. "No law broken here. Maybe a little disagreement between husband and wife. Maybe even a divorce for him lying to me. If I had enough time, that is."

"Hon," Roy grabbed his wife's hand. "You're going to take the word of a garbage man over your own husband?"

"What am I missing here?" Wade asked, once again fiddling with his handcuffs. "If there's no law being broken, why am I chained to this chair?"

The woman sat upright and reached for a glass of water, which her husband helped with getting the straw to her mouth. "I asked him to do it. I want him to eat me. Before I die."

Wade shook his head, fearful he had some brain injury that was making him hear delusional words. "I think I need a doctor. Maybe I have brain damage or something."

After a long coughing session, she quit drinking and laid her head back on the pillow. "You promised me, Roy! You swore you were eating it! That's my last wish. For you to eat me before the cancer does. But now I learned you threw it out! You know how bad it hurt? Me slicing off my own breast tissue!"

"Yeah, I have a brain injury for certain," Wade said real low, almost inaudible. His voice got stronger. "I need a doctor, like soon. Please, just let me go!"

"I know it sounds weird, but Mary here has always been fascinated with the works of Marquis de Sade, which isn't a fair representation. Vorarephilia? Gynophagia? Dolcett? The comics? Any of these ringing any bells?"

"The only bells ringing are in my ears," Wade said matter-of-factly. "I think I'm hearing weird stuff. My brain isn't working right."

After another coughing fit, Mary turned to face Wade. "It's not illegal if I ask my husband to eat me. I cut away the flesh for him. He cooked it. I watched him eat it. I'm dying anyway, so it was the perfect opportunity to live out my dream. Of him eating me. But then this knucklehead threw it out with the trash."

"Honey," Roy showed concern in his voice. "I cut it up into small pieces, what you saw me with, it was pork. I can't eat you. It's just not right. I had to watch while you mutilated yourself. Not only do I have to watch my wife die, but should I also watch you kill yourself? It's bound to get infected and kill you before the cancer."

"Like I said. I'm filing for divorce. Unless-" Mary rubbed her tired eyes. "Do you want to make it up to me?"

"Anything to make you happy."

"I want to eat him."

"Honey, I can't kill our garbage man, even if he is worthless. I'll go to prison."

"You can't, but I can," Mary replied with an evil smile painted across her face. "We'll even video it. I have an idea that will make you completely innocent. Knock him out. Please. It's my last wish. As a dying woman."

Wade was screaming *no* as Roy reluctantly made his way towards him with a syringe in his hand.

"I'm so sorry," Roy said as he stuck the needle in his neck. "If you're married, you should know that the wife always gets what the wife wants."

+++++

When Wade opened his eyes, he was the one lying in the hospital bed. His arms and legs were spread out like an 'X', each limb handcuffed to the corresponding parts of the bed.

Shock was the first feeling his brain registered, then it was pain, coming from his leg.

Mary was now sitting next to the bed, her teeth stained red with a floppy piece of meat dangling from her lips. After ripping off a piece of flesh by biting down and wiggling her head side-to-side, she licked her fingers, making loud sloppy, slurping noises. "Yeah, pipe down over there, Roy." As she spoke, she continued to chew, revealing pieces of Wade's masticated thigh. "I know you don't want me doing this. But what are they going to do? Put me in prison? I'll be dead in a week. Big deal."

"It's not too late, honey. You can still let him loose," Roy said, while playing it up and staring into the camera on a table. "Free me from the handcuffs. I'll let him go."

"Nope. I'm already mad at you for not eating me when I offered myself to you. I thought that would be my way of becoming a part of you, forever, even after my death. But no, you had to throw it away. I might end up shooting you, anyway, just for that."

"Wait?" Roy's tone changed from acting, to being serious and solemn. "You don't mean that, do you?"

Mary picked up the gun and aimed it at her husband. "Try me. You're right, he's too raw. Too chewy. Not at all what I expected."

There was enough slack in the handcuffs, that Wade sat up and looked down at his thigh to see a large chunk removed, it leaking blood on the sheets. The array of colors from superficial to deep wound was amazing. If it didn't hurt so bad, Wade would have appreciated the various shades of reds, pinks, purples and even some grays. "No!"

"I knew I should have gagged him!" Mary exclaimed. "Can't a woman try to enjoy her last meal in peace? I knew our BDSM lifestyle would come in handy one day, having all different types of cuffs. Why didn't I think of grabbing a ball gag?"

"If you let me go, I won't tell anyone, I swear!" Wade begged. "I'm so sorry I looked through your trash!"

"I bet you are," Mary said, taking another bite with a sip of water. She was now hunched over, tired from the activities of slicing and chewing. "Good thing for you, I'm so tired."

"I was trying to save you!" Wade rationalized. "All of this was to save you!"

"Save me? From what? My fetishes? My cancer? Nobody can help me now. Nor you."

Mary held up a fork, which had a tidy piece of meat on it. "Roy, do you want to try some?"

Her husband's face almost turned green, and his cheeks blossomed out like a chipmunk.

"That's a no, I guess. What about you, Mr. Garbage Man? You want to taste yourself? Spoiler alert. You're dying no matter what. Do you at least want to die with the taste of human meat on your tongue?"

"What? Why would I do that? You're a psychopath!"

"Roy, over there," Mary looked over her shoulder towards her husband, "was supposed to eat my boob. He didn't, apparently."

"Leave me out of this. I'm just a man over here, being forced to watch my wife commit cannibalism. And no, I couldn't eat you. I just couldn't."

"You afraid of catching my cancer or something? I'm pretty sure it's not contagious. Not even if you consume me."

"There you go again! Can't you stop talking about dying! I know what you're going through, but I'm going through it, too! I'm losing my wife. I have to carry on after you die. And prison life isn't for me!"

Watching husband and wife bicker put thoughts into Wade's mind. "Hey, I'll eat you. What if I eat you? Will you let me live?"

"Can't," Mary said while she shrugged with a mouthful of thigh meat. She leaned down towards the bed, to whisper so the camera couldn't hear her. "You'd tell them he drugged you. Knocked you out. I can't let him get in trouble."

"I won't tell anyone! I swear! If I'm on camera eating you, I surely don't want that getting out! I'm a role model for this community. Nobody wants their trash collector to be a known cannibal."

Mary's eyebrows rose, like she was deep in thought. "What about your leg?"

"It's not so bad," Wade lied. "You're a dying woman. I think you should get your final wish."

'Hey! What are you talking about over there?" Roy screamed to be heard.

"Not much, Roy," Wade leaned so that he was looking at the camera. "I'm letting your wife eat my leg so I only think it's fair if I get to eat a piece of her."

"You're good," Mary noted. "Yeah, that works for me. Just leave Roy out of this."

"Roy is obviously an outstanding citizen, doing what he can to stop anything illegal. Teach me about this, uh, Marquis Dolcett thing."

Being weak and only able to barely hold her head up, Mary laid her head on the bed. "Well, it's sexual. It gets my juices pumping, if you know what I mean. My panties are wet now, from eating you. But I'm in no shape to act on my urges. If only I had gotten cancer in my younger days…"

Her words trailed out, leaving a brooding cloud of silence in the room. "I can please you. I can eat you, and then eat you. If you want. You won't have to do any of the work. Just let me free."

"Nope. Nuh-uh," Roy said. "You can eat her, but leave the sex out of it. That's my job!"

"Ignore him," Mary said, smiling at Wade, but then turned with a look of disgust towards her husband. "You had your chance last night. You want me to shoot you?"

++++++++

Mary laid her left hand on the edge of the bed, putting her forearm on display, wrist down. "I'm not sure if this'll be the same as my husband doing it, but it is a lifelong dream. One that I finally get to live."

After taking a pain pill, and drinking some form of medication in liquid form from a glass bottle, Mary's feeble right hand shook with a blade gripped in her fingers.

As the tip of the blade inserted her flesh, Mary's eyes slanted in pain and caused her wrinkles to deepen. A soft grunt escaped her lips, gurgled with a phlegm-like sound.

The paring knife wasn't large, but it was sharp and perfect for precision.

A thin line of red leaked from her, creating a small stream that would forever stain the white bedsheets.

Wade couldn't help but feel her dedication to her cause, emotionally.

Once the tip was buried in her forearm, she flattened the knife, and began to slice away a thin layer, pulling the knife horizontal of her arm.

Wade's eyes widened as she dragged the sharp metal through herself, peeling away a thin layer.

"It'll be like bacon," she explained, her eyes barely wincing with pain. "I'll use my lighter to char it lightly. At the very least, it will burn away the hairs."

True to her word, she did just that, her arm flesh dangling from the prongs of a fork. She tried to raise her lighter with her other arm, but between the medication, open wound, and lethargy, it was an impossible task.

"If I undo one of your arms, can you do the lighter?"

"Sure." Wade knew this would be his opportunity to break free. Internally, he was struggling between escaping, but knew his selfishness would ruin a dying woman's last wish.

Mary fumbled for the key which she had buried beneath her thigh, and unlocked one of his hands, her own shaking. After unlocking one of the cuffs, she dropped the key, not bothering to look and see where it landed on the carpet.

His moral code kicked in, and Wade knew he should please her. It was the least he could do. With his uncuffed hand, he flicked the flame to life. With several up-and-down motions, he lightly cooked the meat.

The hairs curled as if they were trying to retract back to their origin root follicle.

The smell, like a combination of cooking pork and rubber tires burning out on pavement, fascinated Wade. The odor was strong enough to even break through his nose blindness.

"I want to watch you eat me," Mary said through labored breathing.

"Hon, you're wearing yourself out. You need to get back in bed and rest."

"Shut up, Roy! Please, this one last request." Mary's voice sounded weak and indifferent, but her face was lit up with anticipation.

In her efforts to get comfortable, Mary laid the blade on the bed, but never took her eyes off Wade as he brought the fork to his mouth. Her flesh, semi-blackened, did look like an undercooked piece of bacon flapping as it came closer to Wade's mouth.

His teeth were firm and strong enough to break off a piece. An explosion of blood traversed his tongue, coating all of his taste buds. It was unlike anything he had ever experienced before. Wade smiled, and complimented her. "You're delicious. Absolutely a taste of joy."

"Yeah! Yeah!" Mary got excited and raised her head with a smile.

Her eyes bulged out of her head as a coughing fit overtook her.

It sounded like she was hyperventilating, but without as much force as one would expect. The panting was a rotation of gasping and blowing, ending with heaving.

A slight moan followed, and Mary's body went limp, her face burying itself in the bed sheets.

"Mary! Mary!" Roy cried out. "Help her," the man pleaded. Being the concerned husband he was, Roy jumped out of the chair, his hands dragging the furniture with him as he maneuvered across the room the best a man can do while dragging a heavy item behind him. "You killed my wife!"

Wade made himself as small as he could on the bed, and wished he could curl into a ball and cover his ears so that he wouldn't have to listen to the heartbreak in Roy's voice.

"She's dead!" Roy cried, now stroking his wife's corpse face.

"She's smiling, though," Wade offered in sympathy. "She died happy."

It took minutes, but Roy's tears faded.

"Hey, I have an idea," Wade said once it was silent. "If I know anything, it's how to dispose of stuff."

Roy looked at him confused, but listened to Wade's plan.

+++++

Wade's bandaged leg ached as he climbed on the rear step of the garbage truck. With antibiotic cream, and simple soap and water, he was keeping his open wound as clean as possible, even while I'm on the job, ensuring to not spill any garbage on his pants.

A familiar house was coming up on his route, and Wade couldn't help but smile, recalling his adventure over the weekend.

Once he reached Mary's house, he knew what was in the bags, and wasn't surprised when the bones clinked together with a cluttering sound.

By the time he and Roy had finished with her, most of her meat had been carved away, stored in freezer bags…

That is what they didn't eat of her.

By the time they finished, all that was left of her were bones.

Wade smiled, knowing that even Roy gave into Mary's last wish. It may have been after her death, but after Wade convinced him how tasty she was, Roy was happy to taste her for himself.

The garbage man threw what few remains there were of Mary into the back of the truck with a smile on his face, knowing that Mary was also smiling down on him, from wherever she ended up.

+++++

A note from the dark mind of Sea Caummisar

I've always been fascinated by vore aka vorarephilia. Also, could be known as gynophagia if a female is being consumed, or androphagia if the specimen is male.

By definition, vorarephilia is the erotic desire to consume or be consumed.

'Soft vore' is basically being eaten alive or whole. 'Hard vore' is known as there being gore or killing involved.

I am by no means an expert on the subject... It's just that rare fetishes interest me.

Most of what I know of the subject stems from comics by an artist by the name of Dolcett (well, he or she is known by that pseudonym but I'm pretty sure the actual identity is anonymous). In those stories, usually female subjects, were killed by their own request and eaten in a sexual cannibalistic manner.

These are the topics that my dark mind wonders about and even checks out on the internet. Maybe that's part of the reason I'm told that I have a dark mind.

I wanted to combine vore with a dying woman (cancer), a husband in denial, but the wife finding a willing subject.

Why did my mind make the willing party a garbage man? I don't know, even a mystery to me, but then Wade was born into my library of fictional characters.

Is vore true? Has there ever been anyone to actually do this? Probably so.

Is it illegal for someone to carve out their own meat and offer it to you to eat? I'm not a lawyer so I can't say. If I were a betting person, there are laws and possibly health codes that would be violated in the consumption of human flesh.

DO NOT TRY THIS AT HOME

A Few Previously Published Works

Intro to 'PGAD Anxiety'

This happens to be one of my favorites, but it just so happens that this story was rejected several times. What does a writer do when they wrote something they love, but can't find a publisher to include it in one of their anthologies?

The author publishes it as a bonus short story following one of their own works.

I should apologize to the readers who have read 'The Absence of Pain' because after a few years of not finding a home for this short, it ended up as back matter there.

Rejection is part of being a writer, and I got to the point that I was rejected so many times that I don't even submit to anthologies anymore. Several that rejected this story were non-paying anthologies. Yeah, that hurt. Am I bitter? Nope. Maybe I'm realistic that the shortest way from A-Z is to publish it myself.

If you're reading this, I know you're a reader that found me and gave me confidence in my writing voice. Most publishers hate my stuff, but as long as kewl people like you keep reading, I'll keep writing.

For those not familiar with PGAD (persistent genital arousal disorder), it's a rare condition in which one gets sexually aroused for no reason and even an orgasm can't cure that feeling. An episode can last days, and sometimes even weeks. From what I researched, it can drive a person mad.

If you've read it before, feel free to skip over the next 2,000 words.

If you haven't, I hope you enjoy.

The end notes from the dark mind of Sea Caummisar

sjsjs

PGAD Anxiety

Eve was only a teenager when she was first diagnosed with PGAD (persistent genital arousal disorder). During the initial episode, she didn't know what was happening with her body. It occurred when she was standing in her high school English class giving an oral book report. While she was speaking and looking at her classmates, her body started *changing.*

Since she was so young then, sex was a brand-new experience for her. Eve felt her panties get moist, and the pressure making her vaginal lips swell was very uncomfortable. The urge to stick her hand down her pants and scratch herself was very tempting, but she knew better than to do that in front of an audience. Instead, she chose to excuse herself to the restroom.

Eve's first orgasm was when she was standing all alone in a dirty bathroom stall not even touching herself.

Her mother called the disease the handiwork of Satan, even though doctors persisted otherwise. It was a disease of the body. Spontaneous orgasms led to a life of panic attacks and depression for Eve. After being exposed to electroconvulsive therapy the disease subsided and hadn't resurfaced for many years.

Now, ten years later, the disease came back. Eve laid in bed after masturbating for the seventh time today. Not even inducing an orgasm would lessen the feeling of pins and needles in her sexual area.

After seeing several doctors and trying new medicines nothing seemed to lessen her episodes anymore. There was not an antidepressant in the world that could make her feel better about this unusual disease. Being sexually aroused for no reason, and for extended amounts of time took a toll on the mind and body.

This attack had lasted for nearly four hours. Sometimes they could last days. Even though orgasms make most people happy, too much of anything is a bad thing. At first, she tried not touching herself, but the pain only got worse. Now that she had resorted to masturbating, her clitoris was rubbed raw and painful to touch.

Finding no relief, Eve's mind taunted her. There had to be a way to make her symptoms subside. Being constantly aroused with your vaginal lips engorged with blood would take its toll on even a sane person. The medicine wasn't working, so she poured another glass of bourbon to help ease the pain.

She had tried sticking dildos inside her, even ones that vibrated. That only made her body happier and would result in her squirting her sexual fluids on her bedsheets. Cold cucumbers didn't work either. All it did was partially numb the walls of her vagina (temporarily), yet she would still be aroused.

At one point, the pain was so bad that she considered taking a handful of sleeping pills just to escape the harsh reality of never-ending sexual arousal. Even though Eve knew that was her depression talking, it still seemed to be a valid solution. Instead, she poured another glass of bourbon and took a sip of the one thing that could possibly make her feel better.

Since she didn't want to take such drastic measures, Eve tried touching herself again to relieve some pressure. Sliding her finger between her lips, she realized that she was tighter than ever. The pressure from the blood and being swollen made it almost impossible to get her digit inside her cavity.

Layers of secreted juices had built up from her past orgasms. The squishing sounds of the fluids oozing out of her was disgusting. Eve's anus collected the overflowing moisture. Once again, her bedsheets were soaking wet.

As she scraped the sides of her vaginal cavity, her thumb brushed against her tender clit. Another wave of orgasms sent pleasure impulses down her body that border lined on pain.

The muscles of her womanhood squeezed so tight that her finger was stuck inside her. Eve tried to relax and calm herself down, knowing that was the only way she would ever get the use of her hand back. Taking deep breaths, she exhaled through her nose.

    As she pulled her hand free, a suctioning noise spilled her sexual juices onto the bed. Still, her body begged for more. She realized she was a slave to her vagina, and that it would never be pleased.
    Even though Eve had no sexual appetite, her body craved it, needed it. Her sore clitoris begged to be touched as her vaginal cavity contracted once again. Another climax. She laid on the bed, which was covered in sweat and her own female ejaculate.
    In the attempt to shake off her dirty feeling, Eve hopped in the shower and let the water cleanse her of her own filth. The water sprinkled on her body like raindrops. As it hit her clitoris, painful sensations radiated across her tender region. Turning her back to the water, she watched as her thick juices dripped onto her feet.
    The warm water of the shower seemed to sober her up a little bit. The alcohol was easing the pain a bit, but not enough to subside the aches of her woman parts.
    After getting as clean as she could, Eve decided it was time to take charge of her own body. She was willing to do what needed to be done to be rid of Satan's handiwork (as her mother called it). Even if it meant taking drastic measures. Drastic times called for drastic

measures, so she turned the bourbon bottle upside down, taking a long swig.

As her southern regions throbbed, the pressure building up in her loins dropped her to her knees. Eve cried out in pain, but there was nobody around to hear her cries for help. Tears fell down her face like rain pouring from a dark cloud. Since the pain was already unbearable, even hurting herself worse would be a quick fix to her current situation.

Her drunken mind informed her of a permanent solution.

Eve stumbled into the kitchen for the tools she would need to perform a minor surgery on herself. Scissors and knife seemed appropriate.

Squeezing the thinner, inner vaginal lips (labia minora) she tried to force the fluid out of her skin. They were so engorged with blood and looked like pink, plump slabs of beef. With each painful throb, her mind told her to fix herself.

Without even thinking, Eve used her cooking scissors to make a tiny slit on top of both lips. Blood flowed like a stream, but the pressure wasn't as bad as it was.

Closing her eyes and gritting her teeth, Eve spread her inner lips apart and used the scissors to free them from her body. One by one, two tiny pieces of flesh fell on her kitchen floor, making a faint thump sound. The blood that was engorging her sex organ was now spilling onto her feet.

After getting a little light-headed, Eve made her way to her bed to lay down. Since some pressure was gone, walking was easier. Blood continued to drain, even when she was horizontal. She didn't care if her mattress was stained, all she cared about was not feeling aroused anymore.

Even though her inner lips were gone and not hurting as bad as they were before, her outer lips were still throbbing. Since they were too thick to cut completely from her body, Eve chose to

make several small stab wounds with the tips of her scissors, so that any fluid inside of them could also flow freely.

Finally, Eve's mind thanked her for taking the first steps to making herself feel better. However, it reminded her that other parts of her vagina still ached with pain.

Eve took a moment to embrace the pain that wasn't as bad as it had been before. She knew that any wounds she caused to herself could heal with time. Perhaps, it would teach her body a lesson and it would never put her through this torture again.

Even though she had mutilated herself until it looked like she had been mauled by a dog, her vaginal cavity still contracted. Despite everything she had done, her body still craved sex.

Then, a faint throb started again in her clitoris. The angry blades of the scissors easily ate through the tiny organ. As she pulled the scissors to her face, she saw the tiny mass perched atop the scissors.

"I bet you won't do this to me again."

Even though she had officially lost her mind because she was talking to her detached parts of her

sexual organ, Eve didn't care. The pain from her self-mutilations was nowhere near as bad as the episodes of PGAD (persistent genital arousal disorder).
    After all the orgasms she had experienced, Eve never wanted to have another one in her life. The blood started flowing thicker and heavier, but she didn't care. All she cared about was not hurting anymore.

    The interior walls of her vaginal cavity still contracted, reminding her of how horny her body still was. She wasn't sure how she could remove the inner walls of her vagina, but she was determined to figure it out.
    As she walked from her bed to the bathroom, a trail of blood dripped from in between her legs. Soon, her thighs were a crimson red color. She knew that the cold temperatures of a cucumber provided brief relief, and wondered what heat would do.
    Eve eyed her curling iron, and it seemed to be a perfect match. Not only was the cylindrical shape perfect to fit inside of her, she had also heard that heat promotes healing properties. Surely, this would give her some pain relief.
    Eve watched the blood drip on the floor as she waited for the curling iron to heat up. Seconds felt like hours as the pins and needles feeling inside of her reminded her of her condition.
    As soon as the curling iron was hot to the touch, Eve placed it near the entry of her womanhood. Each drop of blood on the hot metal plates made sizzling

noises. She anticipated how great it would feel to punish her sexual organ for mistreating her.

Since her muscles were still tight from having orgasms, Eve had to slowly glide the curling iron inside of her.

Skin sizzled and juices made bubbles coming out from her innards. The smell of burnt sex was nothing that she had ever experienced before. She tried to stop herself from retching, but she couldn't. Bile rose from her stomach and she spewed chunks of her lunch into her bathroom sink.

She could feel the heat cooking her womb, but it did make her muscle contractions ease a little bit. The warmth radiated all the way to her navel, and streaks of red lines littered her pubic region. As she pulled the tool out from her, chunks of black skin stuck to the metal plates.

Finally, when she laid down, she was no longer horny. There was pain, but it wasn't as bad as it had been earlier. Sleep was the only thing her body craved now. As soon as she closed her eyes, a familiar faint throb grew inside of her.

"No! I can't take it anymore!" Eve cried.

Even though she had cut off her thin vaginal lips, punctured holes in her thicker lips, removed her clitoris, and burnt her vaginal cavity, her body still needed sex.

Eve grabbed the knife, ready to put it to use. She knew the only way to fix herself was to fully remove as

much of her vagina as she could. She slowly pulled back her outer lips, and
quickly glided the knife into them. One by one, they fell onto her bedsheets, spilling even more of her blood.

Then, as careful as she could, Eve placed the blade inside of her. As she scraped any tissue she could from her vaginal walls, she started to feel relief. Soon, her wrist twisted the knife in a circular motion to ensure she removed every part of her vagina that she could.

As she used her fingers to spoon out burnt, bloody vaginal samples, Eve was feeling better. The charred pieces of flesh smelled like overcooked fish. The blood they were soaked in made them slippery to the touch.

Once again, her brain begged for sleep. Eve closed her eyes, and was finally comfortable enough to get some rest. Little did she know, she had lost too much blood and would never open her eyes again. At least now, and forever, she would never be sexually aroused, ever again.

End

Intro to 'Worst Fear'

I don't poke around on social media too often, but when I do, it's usually book related. There's a great FB group dedicated solely to horror books, and that's one of the online groups that I truly enjoy.

That leads me to one of my tamer stories previously published in 'Books of Horror Community Anthology Vol 1' (2020).

I met these wonderful people online, readers and writers, and I can tell you from experience that this group makes you feel welcome the moment you join.

When someone proposed the idea of putting together an anthology of writers (new and old).... Well, I submitted a story. The PGAD story. It was rejected.

Being rejected by a non-paying gig isn't fun, but I wanted to be included, which is something rare for me. I'm not the kind of person that needs the approval of others, but I was persistent. I submitted a tamer story, and they chose to publish this one in their anthology.

It's probably one of my least favorite works, but some people seem to enjoy it.

Worst Fear

The unsettling taste in her mouth was bile. It took every bit of will she had within her to fight the urge to vomit. Letting last night's dinner out might have made her feel better, but it would also be a sign of weakness.

She could feel the hate radiating from her tormentor's body as he stood behind her, holding two blades in his hands. His long blades reflected the bright lights that illuminated the room. At the end of each knife was a sharp point that could easily puncture her skin. They were the sharpest blades she had ever seen in her whole life.

The event had started simple enough when he forced her into the chair. The moment the chair started to squeak and he spun her around was when she knew there was danger.

Paralyzed by fear, her body wouldn't respond to her movements. No matter how hard she told her limbs to move, they wouldn't. Knowing that she needed to force herself to stand up and fight and flee for her life made things worse. Her mind became her own worst enemy.

Anxiety kicked in, her heart pounding loudly in her chest. She could feel her pulse throbbing throughout her body as her blood pressure rose. Her tormentor slapped a noose-like tarp around her neck and she could feel her neck constricting. The tarp was too tight. It gripped around her throat feeling like fingers strangling the life out of her body.

Feeling like she could no longer breath contributed to her body disobeying her. The tarp covered the entirety of her body and she knew the bad person planned on things getting messy. Why would he want to protect her body from what was to come next?

Her eyes widened as she realized there was a mirror right in front of her. What kind of sick-o would force a person to watch their own torture?

In her reflection, she could see her fear seeping out of her pores. Sweat trailed from her forehead, running down her cheeks.

For whatever reason that she couldn't move was a mystery to her. The man seemed nice enough when she met him. Had he poisoned her with something?

He held the blades above her head and smiled. She knew he was a monster when he told her to calm down and to slow her breathing. The nerve of that man! To actually ask her if she was okay.

The mirror she was forced to stare into showed that she obviously wasn't okay. Being covered in sweat and on the verge of crying should have been clues that he didn't need to ask her.

The world was spinning at a microscopic pace. Everything was happening in slow motion. The man moved slowly as he held both blades close to her head.

Forcing her eyes closed, she refused to watch. After waiting for what felt like an eternity and saying silent prayers in her head, she felt nothing.

She heard a faint noise, something indecipherable.

After opening one of her eyes just a bit, she saw pieces of herself being cut off, forever removed from her body.

Since she didn't feel any pain, she knew that she must have been drugged.

Once again, she closed her eyes. What she saw in the blindness was her imagination playing tricks on her. Distorted illusions of the blades snipping her ears from her head were just as bad as what she saw in reality.

Did the man plan to scalp her? Would this be his trophy that he could display on his wall to forever remember this moment?

She tried hard to not think about what he planned to do with the pieces he had removed from her.

"Open your eyes and look."

Fearing to disobey the cruel man, she opened her eyes. Her head looked different in a way that she couldn't describe. There were so many pieces of her on the ground that she started to cry. Large tears fell from her face onto the tarp that was covered with small pieces of herself.

"It's okay." The cruel man spoke calmly. "You just sit and relax. I'm just about done here."

Her mind raced to figure out what he meant by done? Would that be the finale? Did that mean the next step was death?

She didn't want to die. There were so many experiences in life that she wanted to explore before she perished. Traveling was something she always wanted to take up, but never did. The things she regretted right before her death seemed silly but she didn't know what else to think about.

It was too painful to think about the family she would be leaving behind. Her children would have to live life without a mother. How could her husband raise two small children by himself?

Even though her eyes were open, she wasn't looking at the man as his knives continued to cut into pieces of her.

A wave of nausea struck her. The bile hung in her throat and tasted like rotten sewage. At this point, she felt detached from her body. She didn't feel her cheeks as they swelled up but she could see them expand, holding in the contents of her last meal.

Her body reacted automatically, forcing it back down. The taste was worse than when it had come up. Slime forced itself down her throat, having a hard time trying to get past the point where the thing was tied around her neck.

Not wanting to look in the mirror any longer, she looked to her feet. On the floor lay all of the cruel man's snippings. Larger tears fell down her face.

"It's not that bad, is it?" The old man asked.

She couldn't form words. Did he actually expect her to respond? What was she supposed to say in a situation like this?

All she wanted to do was scream and yell, but it was too late. Her mouth was incapable of producing words. There was no voice left in her dying body.

Still watching her feet, she saw the man shuffle from side to side. His shoes were covered with tiny pieces of her.

She had to face reality and realize that those pieces now belonged to him. They were lost from her body, no longer belonging to her.

Why would this man do this to her? How many other people had he exposed to his torturous ways? How could he find pleasure while cutting up fellow human beings? He had to be a monster. There was no other explanation.

There was evidence on the floor that others had come before her. Their shades were darker than her own. The man didn't even bother to clean up the mess from the ones before her. Did he do that on purpose to make her fear him even more?

"Honey, it's okay."

He was mocking her with his words. She was not okay and never would be again.

"It's over." The old man proclaimed.

Was she dead? She didn't feel dead. She could still hear him.

So, what did over mean? Would she be forced to live the rest of her life scarred by today's events? Would he allow her to keep her life?

Not being as appreciative of her life as she should have been, she vowed that if he allowed her to live, she would travel the world. All of the regrets she had earlier she could rectify.

She could feel the thing around her neck loosen. After inhaling precious oxygen into her lungs, she watched as the tarp's messy contents fell to the floor.

More pieces of herself mixed in with the others.

How body moved now, and she rubbed her throat, making it feel better after being choked for so long.

Amazed by her body movements, she realized that whatever he drugged her with must have worn off.

Feeling no pain and better than she expected, she sat very still, trying to process what had just happened to her.

The old man grabbed a broom and started sweeping around her feet, collecting the pieces.

"Honey, you're okay. And I have other people waiting for a haircut. So if you don't mind."

She looked in the mirror. The dead ends had been removed from her hair. Nothing more. She was alive and well.

With a new appreciation of life, she made her way home.

Tonsurephobia: the fear of getting a haircut.

This is a very real fear that causes anxiety for many people. This is what they experience when they get their haircut.

Intro to Drabbles

What's a drabble? A short fictional story, sometimes exactly 100 words long.

That sounds crazy, right? What kind of story can be told in exactly 100 words? I took that as a challenge. When the Macabre Ladies (publisher) asked if I wanted to try my hand at short fiction, I accepted.

I already told you about my past with being rejected, so I submitted several drabbles for the Macabre Ladies 'Dark Xmas Holiday Drabbles: 100 Word Holiday Horror Stories' (2019).

Silly me, submitted probably too many 100 word horrors, and they accepted every single one of them.

They're short. Fun. And they're all Xmas related. I always planned on writing a Christmas story and adding them in the back matter, but never have, so these drabbles get mixed in here. Even if it's not the holiday season (I am writing this in Nov 2022, so it's almost holiday season here, but it won't be when I release Painbows in March. My bad.)

100 words Xmas Drabbles

The First Signs of a Serial Killer

The five year old boy worked hard on the candy cane, all day.
Each lick and suck of the candy served its purpose.
Even though he didn't care for peppermint, he knew it had to be done.
His mother sat him on Santa's lap, so he could tell him his wish list.
He had no list.
Instead, the young boy stabbed Santa with the sharp shaped point he chiseled on the candy stick.
All he wanted was to see Santa bleed.
He was sad when the candy broke and barely punctured Santa's skin.

A Perfect Snowman

All she needed was a Santa hat to top her perfect snowman.
She glanced at the blue eyes, which she plucked from her husband's head.
The nose looked like it was running, but instead of snot it was blood.
From where she cut it from her husband's face.
The smile didn't look very friendly since the severed lips turned pale and frozen.
Her husband had been moving when she sliced the meat from around his mouth.
So the cuts were jagged.
After adding the Santa hat, it was perfect.
Her husband would never cheat on her again.

A Bad Child

A trail of bloody gingerbread cookies led the young girl to her prizes.
Waking up Christmas Day was always so exciting.
Every year, Santa left behind the best presents.
The green Christmas tree was now red, covered with a sticky liquid.
Full of vigor, the girl didn't want to wait for her parents to wake up.
She opened the first box and her Mother's head was inside, scary blank eyes staring back into her own.
Krampus appeared behind her, holding up his bloody claws, grinning wide and showing his pointed red teeth.
"Were you naughty this year?"

Rudolph the Bloody Nosed Reindeer

Rudolph the bloody nosed reindeer.
Had such a bloody nose.
And if you ever saw it, you would even say it shows.

All of the other reindeer used to hit him and call him names.
That's why poor bloody Rudolph made up his own reindeer games.
Then one foggy Christmas Eve, Santa came to say
"Rudolph with your broken nose so bloody, do you want to play your games tonight?"
That's why the reindeer hated him, and they ran away to flee.
Rudolph the bloody nosed reindeer:
His reindeer massacre went down in history.

Shiny Ornaments

Shiny ornaments dangle from the green Christmas tree.
Shiny ornaments make the Christmas tree so pretty.
Shiny ornaments silver, gold, red and green.
Shiny ornaments so fragile.
Shiny ornaments made of thin glass.
Shiny ornaments break so easily.
Shiny ornaments crush so easily.

Shiny ornaments I envision smashing in the faces of my family.
Shiny pieces of shiny ornaments eating deep into their skin.
Shiny pieces of shiny ornaments stuck in the faces of my family.
Shiny blood on the shiny ornaments.
Broken shiny ornaments dangle from the Christmas tree.
Shiny blood dripping from the broken shiny ornaments.

Intro to Flash Fiction

After having those 100 word drabbles published in the 100 word Dark Xmas drabbles, the Macabre Ladies moved on to Valentine's Day. I'm a sucker for love. I love love. You probably can't tell that by the dark things I write about, but I'm a hardcore romantic.

I've been happily married to the love of my life for more years than I care to disclose because that will really show my age!!! LOL> but I couldn't imagine life without him. I know it's corny, but I don't think I could exist without him. To have that true feeling, the one that you just know and just feel, that you've met the one that completes you. It's amazing.

Yeah, I know, I couldn't be any more cliché. But it's true. He makes me who I am and a better person.

Enough sappy crap already, let's move onto to something more interesting.

This was a piece published in an anthology ('Dark Valentine Holiday Horror Collection: A Flash Fiction Anthology') and was flash fiction and my challenge was to write a love story in 500 words.

Blood Wine

Jarod was sweet enough to hold the door open as Sandra entered the restaurant. This was his first date since his girlfriend moved out six months ago and he wanted to be sure to do everything perfect. It wasn't everyday that he met a woman on the internet that interested him. Especially with Valentine's Day being their first date, he knew there was pressure to be a perfect gentleman.

As she walked in, Sandra wrinkled her nose. "What is this place again? What am I smelling?"

The hostess interrupted Sandra as she took their reservation and led them to a table. In Sandra's eyes, the place was too dark and unsettling.

As he sat down, Jarod began explaining himself. "A friend told me about this place. It's only open two nights a year. Valentine's Day and Halloween. I saw on your dating profile that you also love old vampire movies. My friend told me about this place and said it's the best."

Sandra fought the urge and repressed her feelings of wanting to run out of the place. Of course, she had to pick a blind date with a guy that only noticed her interest of vampires on her profile. She knew it was risky using a horror dating website, but she also liked the thrill of it.

The already dimmed lights got darker. Nearly naked women covered in red body paint took to the stage. Once again, Sandra caught a whiff of a familiar aroma. The women on stage started wiggling their bodies. The women reached in between their legs and scooped out menstrual blood from their vaginas and rubbed it on each other.

A worker approached their table and set down two wine glasses. "As you can see, I brought two clean needles, unopened. I am licensed to take blood. So will you be drinking your own or each other's?"

Nothing was making sense to Sandra.

"Our own. First date." Jarod nodded.

Still confused, Sandra watched as the worker plunged the needle in her date's arm and let his red fluid drain into his own wine glass. She had to fight the urge to flee, because she was feeling her eye teeth start to grow. (Something she refused to show in public)

Jarod was smiling, but his eyes weren't glowing like his date's red eyes.

He saw his date wasn't smiling. "Too much for you? Is it too over the top? I thought this would impress you."

In the darkness of the room, Sandra allowed her teeth to grow longer. Sandra bit into her wrist and let her own blood flow into her own wine glass. Sandra gave her offering to Jarod.

Her plans of finding another man to drain his body of blood and discard had been foiled. Jarod had actually impressed her. This was a mortal she wouldn't mind sharing her immortality with.

Jarod almost wet his pants as he realized his date was an actual vampire.

See ya next read

Printed in Great Britain
by Amazon